Spangles McNasty

and the Tunnel of Doom

Steve Webb

Illustrated by

Chris Mould

ANDERSEN PRESS · LONDON

First published in 2017 by
Andersen Press Limited
20 Vauxhall Bridge Road
London SW1V 2SA
www.andersenpress.co.uk

2 4 6 8 10 9 7 5 3 1

British Library Cataloguing in Publication Data available.

ISBN 978 1 78344 508 0

Printed and bound in Great Britain by
Clays Limited, Bungay, Suffolk, NR35 1ED

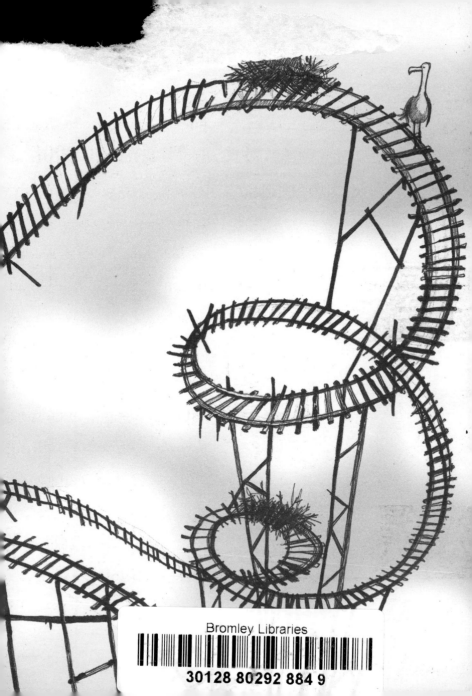

Also out:
Spangles McNasty and the Fish of Gold

For Nutter
(My imaginary dog)

SW

For Steve's left leg

CM

Shiny Times

Spangles McNasty was a right stinker of a rotter of a nasty of a man. The sort of menace who was happiest when he was eating cold chips from bins, shouting at babies, pulling faces at old ladies and farting in the library – preferably all at the same time.

He owned a heart as cold as a penguin's choc ice, a pair of dancing caterpillar eyebrows, a rusty camper van and a baldy head full of nasty dreams. But one thing he did not own was a tie, so he was making one out of tin foil.

Spangles stapled the finished tin-foil tie to his grubby shirt, his eyebrows tangoing expertly across his forehead as he did so. He admired his handiwork in the rear-view mirror of his camper-van home and added a tin-foil moustache, which he attached with sticky tape. The moustache was exactly the same shape and size as his actual for-real handlebar moustache but a bit more shiny and a lot less hairy. Finally, he placed a large tin-foil hat-shaped sculpture on top of his baldy head.

As disguises go, it was a bit rubbish.

Rubbish but shiny and, Spangles hoped, enough to stop the Mayor recognising him.

Spangles had been invited to the reading of a will in Bitterly Town Hall. He didn't know what a 'reading of a will' was but he did know the Town Hall was where the Mayor worked and he didn't think Mayor Jackson would be too pleased to see him.

They didn't really get along.

Spangles thought this was because the Mayor was jealous of his moustache. Mayor Jackson thought it was because Spangles McNasty liked 'collecting' other people's spangly, shiny, glittery things, or as everyone else calls it, 'stealing'.

Adjusting his tin-foil tie a little, Spangles wondered why tin foil was always silver and not gold and momentarily considered inventing it but quickly changed his tiny mind as that would be all kinds of boring compared to collecting stuff.

For now, though, collecting would have to wait. First there was the MYSTERY of the will-reading to solve. He pulled a letter from inside his pin-striped jacket, unfolded it and gave it the stare once more. The stare was Spangles' way of dealing with things he didn't understand. It rarely worked, but it was always worth a try.

THE LAST WILL AND TESTAMENT OF MAGGIE NUGGET

the letter declared in tall shouty capitals across the top. Maggie Nugget was his aunt. So far so good. But a **'Will'** and a **'Testament'**? And the 'last one'? Was it a party? Two dogs: one called Will; the other, Testament?

Spangles' mind was jolted back to its own peculiar reality by a sudden loud banging on the side of his van.

'Wakey, wakey!' Sausage-face Pete yelled, poking his head, hat and beard combination through the window, and filling Spangles' camper van with a **stink of fish** so strong you could spread it on toast.

Spangles twanged the elastic of Sausage's fake beard against his cheek. 'Why do you **always** wear these **fake** whiskers, Sausage?' he asked his old friend with genuine curiosity.

Sausage huffed his head from the window and straightened his oversized yellow fisherman's hat. 'You do know you're dressed like a spaceman, me old rocket ship?' he replied, feeling his feelings a little dented. 'I'll have you know this beard once

belonged to my grandfather **Fish-face Jeffrey**.'
He gave the fake fuzz a stroke, as if it was a family
pet, which was pretty much how he thought of it,
except he hadn't given it a name or its own bed.

Sausage-face Pete had been a fisherman long
enough to become so used to the **smell of fish** he
didn't notice it any more, but everyone else did.
Spangles couldn't help thinking that today the
aroma was particularly strong.

Sausage continued to stroke his fake beard
silently.

'**What are you up to, Sausage?**' Spangles asked.
He could smell a spangly opportunity a mile
away, and a fishy friend even further than that.

Sausage suddenly remembered his news. He
stopped huffing and started bragging instead.

'Well, it's funny you should ask, **me old salt an' vinegar**. You are looking at the owner of Bitterly Bay's newest fish restaurant: **the Sloshy Sushi**,' he announced proudly.

'**Really?** Where is he?' Spangles poked his own head through the window and looked up and down the street.

Sausage ignored his cheeky friend. '**Sushi** is like **normal fish** but **so posh**  you don't have to cook it. Easy peasy, but without the peas,' he explained. 'Opening soon-ish, **free** glass of sea water with every uncooked dead

 fish!' he added, flourishing a hand-drawn poster under Spangles' tin-foil tache.

'Sounds **disgusting**. Count me in.' Spangles snatched the poster and stuffed it into his jacket pocket. 'But first, what do you make of this **jibber jabber** about **wills and things**?' He flapped his own paperwork under Sausage's stinky beard.

Sausage lifted the brim of his hat and peered at the letter. 'Aha!' he exclaimed after a moment's remembering. 'A will reading. I went to one of those when my grandfather stopped hanging around my boat.'

Spangles remembered Sausage's grandfather living on his boat with him for a while before he died. Or was it the other way round? It was Sausage's grandfather's fishing boat and, after he died, it became Sausage's boat. Somehow.

'But it can't be about **my** grandfather. He left years ago,' Sausage said, puzzling at the letter again.

'He didn't leave, Sausage, **he died**,' Spangles said as sensitively as he could.

'I know, I know, it just sounds so **GLOOMY**. I prefers to say he's **swimmin' with the fishies** or **dancin' with the dodos!**'

'**Whatever** you want to call it, he's not 'ere. And what's that got to do with this **will thing**?'

'Well, a will is a sort of list of what dead 'uns want to do with all their stuff after they've died,' Sausage explained, completely delighted to be on the wisdom end of a conversation for a change. He grinned as triumphantly as he imagined Sir Isaac Newton probably did when he worked out what gravity was all about. 'And this will-thing you're going to is about some dead nutter called Maggie Nugget, me old jigsaw puzzle.'

The pieces finally fell into place for Spangles. His aunt Nugget had indeed sadly died. Spangles had even been to the funeral. Almost. He went as close as he could but found the whole thing made him feel very angry and some other feeling he'd never felt before and didn't like one bit.

Or as everyone else calls it: feeling sad.

Now he was **beginning** to feel it again just by thinking about feeling it before.

'You all right there, **me old handkerchief**?' Sausage asked.

'Just got **something** in me eye, Sausage!' Spangles shouted, his mixed-up emotions melting like jelly in custard. Aunt Nugget had **always** been kind to Spangles as a boy. Kind enough to teach him how to cheat at cards, pick pockets and steal just about **anything.**

He smiled at this particular remembering, and suddenly feeling a lorry-load happier said, 'For once, Sausage, I think you might **actually** be right. This **"will reading"** business is something to do with my aunt Nugget and how you got to keep your grandfather's boat.'

'She can't have **my boat**!' Sausage-face Pete suddenly yelled, snatching the letter from Spangles. 'It's a sushi restaurant.'

'No, no, Sausage, it's not about **your** boat. It must be about **her** boat,' Spangles replied calmly, taking the letter back and checking the time of the **will reading** again.

'I didn't know she was a fisherman.' Sausage frowned.

Spangles turned the letter over to show Sausage

his favourite part, the part that said the **will reading** would also reveal who would be the new owner of the Tunnel of Doom. He didn't know what that meant but he liked the sound of it, so he tried it out. **'Someone is about to become the new owner of The TUNNEL OF DOOOOOOOM, Sausage.'**

'Funny name for a boat?' Sausage said.

'Exactly,' Spangles said, striding off in the direction of the Town Hall, **'Exactly!'**

Vinegar's Best Bitter

Freddie Taylor was **SCARED** of heights, so he had his eyes closed. Wendy McKenzie nudged him gently with a pointy elbow as they reached the highest point of the Biggish Wheel. The aptly named **Biggish Wheel** was only slightly taller than the neighbouring helter skelter and seemed, to Wendy at least, a good place for Freddie to start **FACING HIS FEAR.**

The wheel clanked noisily to a halt, causing the seats to rock gently, and Freddie to grip the safety rail even tighter. 'Silly thing to be SCARED of, really,' Wendy said. 'Not as if heights can pick you up by the ankles and eat you for lunch.'

'Or go WHOOOOO in the night,' added Tommy the Ghost, from the seat behind them.

'Or that,' agreed Wendy.

'OK, OK. I get the picture.' Freddie opened his eyes, looked down at his **white-knuckled hands** and tried to relax his grip a little.

'The only consolation of being dead is that you can't die,' Tommy continued, with what he considered to be wisdom from beyond. 'That, and you can work on a **GHOST TRAIN**.'

Wendy turned to face him. He was wearing his work costume, a white sheet with two roughly cut eye holes, 'Tommy, darling, for the millionth time, you don't have to be a **GHOST** to work on a ghost train.'

Tommy the Ghost was convinced that he was actually for-real dead. Despite being perfectly healthy and only eighteen years old, he thought he was a **GHOST**. A ghost that no one could see, except Wendy McKenzie. This, Tommy presumed, was because she was so old she was pretty close to '**the end**' herself. Although that didn't explain why Freddie could see him too. Tommy decided that Freddie must have **PSYCHIC POWERS** which meant he too could see dead people. Powers Freddie must share with a lot of people in Bitterly Bay, now he came to think of it, because pretty much everyone could see him.

'Anyway, if you were dead, you wouldn't be

SCARED of heights, is all I'm saying,' Tommy concluded.

'Not helping,' Freddie replied, now staring straight ahead to the far end of the pier, where the funfair ended with the towering old roller coaster: the **TUNNEL OF DOOM**.

Wendy followed Freddie's gaze. 'Now that's more like it, darling,' she said. 'If you ride the **TUNNEL OF DOOM**, you'll conquer your fears for good.'

'No chance,' Tommy's decidedly un-ghostly voice offered. 'It's **AS DEAD AS I AM**. That old coaster hasn't rolled anyone anywhere for years.'

'I heard the owner died, too. I'm surprised you haven't bumped into her on your ghost train,' Wendy teased. 'She was planning on re-opening it, I think, but only got as far as giving it a new name.'

'Well, it's right next to my ghost train and it's been closed my **WHOLE DEATH**,' Tommy added.

Wendy had invited Tommy along for the ride, hoping to persuade him that he wasn't dead at all, but alive and well. She was by far the oldest, longest-serving tenant of Bitterly Funfair, and felt a sort of motherliness towards all of her fellow funfairers. So far, coaxing **TOMMY THE GHOST** back to the land of the living wasn't going well at all.

'So, Tommy, darling,' Wendy began seriously, 'you think you're a ghost because you work on a ghost train. Correct?'

'I AM A GHOST and I work on a ghost train,' Tommy agreed.

'And all the other ghost trains, they're all operated by ghosts too?' Wendy asked.

'Correct,' Tommy agreed again.

'So all the ghosts of all the people who have ever lived and died since the beginning of time . . . they all work on ghost trains?' Wendy asked, trying to keep a straight face.

Tommy paused. 'Don't be daft, they wouldn't fit. It's something to do with science,' was his unhelpful answer.

Wendy sighed and decided to leave Tommy to his delusions for a minute and enjoy the view.

It was early on a Tuesday morning, so the funfair was almost deserted. Wendy's gaze swept over the beach and along the quiet promenade where she spotted a lone figure looking in a café

28

window. The tall silhouetted man removed his large hat and ducked slightly to fit through the café doorway.

The café was empty. This was not because of the earliness of the o'clock, there were plenty of other cafés in Bitterly Bay and they were all plenty busy. It was because of Vinegar Jones.

Vinegar Jones was the bitterest lady in Bitterly Bay and possibly the Universe. She hated everyone everywhere and very nearly everything, all of the time. The one thing that she did not hate was coffee. Vinegar Jones loved coffee with all of her beans.

She loved the bitter smell and she loved the bitter taste. So much so in fact that she opened a café selling only coffee and called it 'Vinegar's Best Bitter', which as names for cafés go was rubbish. The name scared away most of the customers and she did the rest.

So the café was always empty. Which was just how she liked it.

Vinegar Jones was busy practising scowling at her reflection in the kettle when the door opened. A tall man holding a large hat in his hand stepped in and announced in a very polite and American accent, 'Good morning, ma'am. A mocha frappuccino espresso macchiato latte to go, please.' This particular customer had a very American accent because he was an

American and not an actor and was visiting
Bitterly Bay for the first time.

Vinegar stared at him. She hated him
immediately. She hated his hat and his tallness
and the funny way he talked, all talky-talk-talk
like that.

Ugh, she thought, and ducked behind the counter, sticking her face in a large freshly opened sack of coffee beans. She took a deep breath, filling her lungs with the beautiful bitterness.

'Excuse me, ma'am?' the American gentleman said politely.

Oh how she hated him.

Vinegar stood up, raising two fists full of beans above her head and yelled,

'This is a coffee shop!'

Guy Walker, the American-not-actor, was beginning to regret popping into the café for a coffee on his way to the Town Hall. He checked his watch and decided to leave. He didn't have time for this. Whatever *this* was. '**Have a good day,**' he said, even more politely as he left.

'Get out!' Vinegar Jones screamed after him.

Guy Walker turned to his right and strode on towards the Town Hall, away from the funfair and away from an argument that was erupting at the entrance to the pier.

'You can't stop there, Two-scoops. This is my patch,' Fat Tony shouted angrily from his hot-dog van parked by the entrance gates to the funfair. 'Move it, or you'll get these right up your nose!' he threatened, waving two long, rubbery hot dogs.

Tony Two-scoops and his ice-cream van were new to Bitterly Bay, having arrived just in time for the summer season. This had annoyed Fat Tony, who instantly decided the whole of Bitterly Bay was his patch and no other vans were allowed; no stationery-supplies vans, no knitting-accessories vans and absolutely no ice-cream vans.

Their incessant arguing was already a familiar soundtrack to the summer all over Bitterly Bay.

Two hot dogs slapped against Tony Two-scoops' van, stuck to the windscreen momentarily and slid slowly earthwards as gravity got a grip.

Gravity loves everything, even hot dogs.

Two-scoops glared at the sliding slimers, swiftly scooped a handful of soft mint choc chip from the fridge and hurled it at Fat Tony's fat face, yelling, 'How very dare you, sir!' Even when he was angry, Tony Two-scoops was exceedingly posh.

Wiping the delicious desert from his eyes, Fat Tony reached for the tomato-sauce bottle (economy size) screaming, 'You've asked for it now, posh ice!'

Two-scoops grabbed two of his own sauce bottles, chocolate and raspberry ripple flavour. 'Oh, **duelling**, is it? **Challenge accepted!**' he said, aiming both at his enemy, ready to squeeze.

Fat Tony charged.

Wendy, Freddie and Tommy the Ghost were so enthralled by this performance they didn't notice another tall, funny-hat-wearing gentleman enter Vinegar Jones' café.

Spangles McNasty kicked open the café door and barked, **'Coffee!'**

Vinegar stared at him. She liked him immediately. She loved his hat and his tallness and the funny way he talked, all talky-talk-talk like that. *'Oooooh!'* she thought, and ducked behind the counter, sticking her face in a large freshly opened sack of coffee beans. She took a deep breath, filling her lungs with the beautiful bitterness.

'Weird,' Spangles said. 'You're weird,' he said, louder this time.

Vinegar peeked over the counter. He was still there. Her heart was racing. She stood up, blushing and giggling at the same time, and said quietly, 'This is a coffee shop!'

'Oh, my mistake, I thought it was a spider,' Spangles replied, all sarcasm and smarty pants.

Vinegar Jones collapsed in a fit of giggles. Before she had a chance to say, 'I am Vinegar Jones and I heart you completely with all my beans,' Spangles gave up, left the café, turned to his right and continued walking towards the Town Hall.

The Folder of Truth

The sun shone its little socks off all over Bitterly Bay. Sitting pretty in a curve of coastline between the Jelly Cliffs in the north and Sandylands to the south, Bitterly Bay was the **bestest**, beautifulest and **oddest** town on the planet of Earth. At least that's what the sun thought, and the sun should know because no one else (apart from the moon) has seen all of the towns on Earth since forever.

'So pthththth!' it would probably say if you disagreed, and if it could speak. Which of course it can't.

The sun liked to get up early in the summer. It had been watching Freddie, Wendy and Tommy the Ghost, Fat Tony and Tony Two-scoops all morning, but it was always particularly interested in the shenanigans of **Spangles McNasty**. Its happy heat followed him along the seafront to the Town Hall. *This should be interesting,* the sun thought. *Mayor Jackson's in there.*

Mayor Jackson was a man with big ideas. Big ideas and a bowler hat, which he wore when he wanted to look a little more important and a little taller.

He adjusted the bowler in the mirror of his huge Mayor's suite on the top floor of Bitterly Town Hall. He had a second office on Bitterly Beach, a beach hut to be precise, which he actually preferred, but the business of this particular Tuesday needed a larger, grander, more important space.

His secretary Marjory's voice burst from the intercom on his desk. 'Mayor Jackson, Mayor Jackson!'

'What is it, Marjory?' Mayor Jackson replied,

shuffling important papers **importantly** in his important Mayor's briefcase.

'Can I have a hug? It's just, I'm a little scared,' Marjory replied. She had been watching **SPOOKY COOKY** on her laptop again. It was an online almost-reality show about haunted food. The **GHOSTLY** fry-ups and creepy desserts always made her rather jumpy.

'Marjory, we really don't have time for this nonsense today. What is it you're scared of exactly?' Mayor Jackson asked wearily.

'I'd rather not talk about it in front of your visitor. But let's just say: **P . . . I . . . E . . . S**,' she spelt with a slight tremble in her voice.

43

'Pies?' the Mayor echoed. 'You're scared of pies?'

'Not all of them,' Marjory said, trying to regain a little dignity.

'Anything else?'

'Cakes, trifles, quiches, sausages . . .'

'No, Marjory. I mean, do you want anything else?'

'Oh. Sorry. Yes, Mr McFarnaby the lawyer is here to see you, Mayor.'

'Splendid, send him in,' Mayor Jackson said, and quickly re-adjusted his bowler hat.

An impeccably dressed gentleman strode purposefully into the Mayor's office, extending a hand in readiness for what would definitely be a very firm, important handshake.

'Barnaby McFarnaby, at your service, Mayor.'

'Aha! Mr McFarnaby.' The Mayor leant across his desk and added his own hand to the shake of importance.

Barnaby McFarnaby may have had a silly name but he too had an important briefcase. He clicked it open, slid out a slim folder and laid it carefully on the table.

Glancing at his important pocket watch, which hc only took out on special occasions or to tell thc time, Mayor Jackson said, 'We have a minute before the reading of the will. I don't suppose an important gentleman such as myself could have a quick peek at it before we go in?' He hoped his handshaking had been impressive enough to suggest a little game of important gentlemen's favours.

Barnaby McFarnaby drummed his long lawyer fingers on the folder and politely declined this suggestion, 'I'm afraid that won't be possible, but tell me, Mayor, what exactly is your interest in this particular will?'

Before the Mayor had a chance to reply, Marjory's voice interrupted from the intercom once more. 'A Mr Walker to see you, Mayor.' Guy Walker had to remove his large cowboy hat again and duck slightly to fit through the office doorway.

'Ah, Mr Walker, come in. May I introduce Barnaby McFarnaby.'

'Pleased to meet you both. And, please, call me Guy.' The tall American introduced himself in his genuine American accent, as he was still an American – or 'dude', as the other Americans might say.

'And what brings you to Bitterly Bay, Guy?' Barnaby asked, still drumming his long fingers of the law on the folder containing the will.

'I'm in antiques,' Guy replied simply. 'Funfair antiques to be precise. And I'm very interested in the **TUNNEL OF DOOM** at the end of Bitterly Bay pier.' He was about to explain further when the intercom interrupted once more.

'It's time for the reading, Mayor. You go on through. I'll be all right on my own . . . I think,' Marjory said nervously. **'Oooooh lawks!'** she squealed with a mixture of delight and terror.

A small crowd of **strange strangers** had gathered in the Beach Suite, the largest of the Town Hall's meeting rooms. Mayor

Jackson led Barnaby McFarnaby to his seat at the head of a long table, while Guy chose to stand at the back of the room, as inconspicuously as an almost seven-foot-tall man wearing a large cowboy hat could.

Barnaby took his seat and opened the folder of truth, peering over his tiny wire-framed spectacles at his audience.

He had met all sorts of people at will readings, ranging from genuinely sad relatives to outright greedy thieves, but this lot looked particularly weird. One of them appeared to be wearing a tin-foil hat, tie and moustache combination.

The sooner we start, the sooner we finish and I can get back to some real lawyering, he thought to himself. He took a deep breath and said, 'Ladies and gentlemen, I have here the Last Will and Testament of Maggie Nugget.'

'Who's she?' someone shouted from the back.

'What's a one of them?' asked another confused voice.

Barnaby surveyed his audience again and chose his words carefully, so everyone would understand. 'Maggie Nugget wanted to give some of you some of her stuff, after she died.'

'Ooh, like a zombie!' an excited voice squealed.

'No. Not like a zombie,' Barnaby continued patiently. 'She wrote it down while she was alive. In her *will*.' He emphasised the last word as clearly as possible and held up the folder of truth. He just wanted to get it over with so he could leave.

He began reading the will, as quickly as he could.

'To my best friend, Dorothy Parsnip, I leave my oven gloves.'

'But I'm allergic to kitchens! She knew that,' Dorothy Parsnip moaned.

'To my gardener, Graham Gardener, I leave my binoculars.'

'But I hate looking at stuff that's far away!' Graham Gardener the gardener grumbled.

'And also my house on the cliffs . . .'

'Oooh,' said Graham. 'That's more like it!'

'. . . which fell into the sea last winter.' Barnaby continued reading what was by far the weirdest will he had ever seen.

'To my darts team-mates, Terry, Sherry, and Jerry, I leave all of the fluff from under my bed.'

'What about the **TUNNEL OF DOOM**, mister?'

a random heckler asked.

'Yeah. What about that?' another, unimaginative heckler joined in.

Barnaby turned the page and remembered to his relief there was only one more item in the will.

'And my precious **TUNNEL OF DOOM**, I leave to my favourite nephew, Spangles McNasty.'

The strange strangers all gasped and exchanged a look that seemed to shout, 'WHAT!? YOU MEAN IT ISN'T ME!'

Spangles McNasty didn't know what a TUNNEL OF DOOM was, but he knew it was now *his* TUNNEL OF DOOM and that was enough to make him suddenly shout, 'Would you look at the spangles on that?!'

Mayor Jackson threw his bowler hat of importance on the floor and stamped on it. He had hoped old Mrs Nugget might have left the TUNNEL OF DOOM to Bitterly Bay Council.

And if the council inheriting the roller coaster had been the ideal outcome of the morning's proceedings, Spangles McNasty inheriting it was definitely the worst news possible.

Spangles McNasty was nasty. Everyone knew that.

Spangles McNasty once stole the Mayor's golden speedboat. Nearly everyone knew that.

How could the Mayor now persuade Spangles to sell the old roller coaster to Guy Walker, who would take it back to America and add it to his antique-roller-coaster theme park? No one knew that.

Why did Mayor Jackson want Guy to take the roller coaster away? Not many people knew that.

Well, how else could Mayor Jackson make room on the end of the pier for his latest tourist attraction, 'The Grande Splash Hotel', which would have water slides from the all the bedroom windows into the sea? Mayor Jackson definitely didn't know that.

'She never said she had a nephew!' complained Dorothy Parsnip.

'Or a favourite one!' added Graham.

'Who is he anyway?' asked Terry, Sherry and Jerry.

'He's that guy in the hat standing at the back,' the Mayor said rather rudely through gritted teeth, staring at Spangles. The rubbish tin-foil disguise hadn't fooled him for a second.

'Who, me?' said Guy, surprised and insulted, but hopeful that he might have just been given the roller coaster he so desperately wanted to buy.

'No, no, sorry, Guy. I mean the guy standing next to you.'

Barnaby McFarnaby strode purposefully to the back of the room and presented Spangles with a folder bulging with boring paperwork, and a large exciting bunch of keys with the words **TUNNEL OF DOOM** engraved on the shiny keyring that held them together. Without another word, he continued striding out of the door and out of Bitterly Bay for ever, he hoped.

Spangles instantly dropped the folder of boring into a nearby bin and held the keys up to the office window, to see if they would **spangle**. They did.

Rotten

Spangles McNasty ran like a pelican, gangling along the sunny promenade. As he approached Bitterly Harbour he ripped off his rubbish tin-foil disguise and shouted ahead to Sausage-face Pete aboard his boat, the *Sloshy Sushi*, '**Sausage**, it's collecting time, bring **Double Bad!**'

Sausage-face Pete was busy on deck painting a sign aboard his new restaurant and had got as far as 'Lovely Uncooked Dead Fishies'. But he dropped his paint brush mid-stroke when he heard Spangles, grabbed the tandem bicycle, known as **Double Bad**, and waited on the quayside for Spangles to hop on.

'What's the hurry, me old race track?' Sausage asked as they pedalled furiously along the seafront moments later.

'I don't think my aunt had a boat after all. **Look at these!**' Spangles replied, handing the **TUNNEL OF DOOM** keys over his shoulder to Sausage.

'**Oh.**' Sausage mumbled, 'These are, erm . . . nice.'

'No, no, Sausage, the address! The address on the keyring! **She's given me** the **TUNNEL OF DOOM**. It's at the end of the pier in the funfair.'

'What's a **TUNNEL OF DOOM**?' Sausage frowned and pedalled, or **fredalled**, as it's sometimes known.

'No idea,' Spangles replied. 'She wasn't involved with the funfair when I was little. But I bet it's covered in **spangles**.' They **swerved** around Fat Tony and Tony Two-scoops, who were still fighting on the promenade.

'Can I have a hot dog, please?!' Tommy the Ghost shouted again in frustration. But Fat Tony was too busy screaming at Tony Two-scoops to pay him any attention. Tommy and Freddie were heading for the TUNNEL OF DOOM. After their ride on the Biggish Wheel, Tommy had insisted on showing Freddie just how high the old roller coaster was. He had also insisted they make a slight detour for hot dogs on the way.

'You see the problems being dead causes?' Tommy moaned to Freddie. 'No one can see me.'

'I think Fat Tony's just a little pre-occupied,' Freddie replied, ducking to avoid an ice-cream

missile that splatted against the hot-dog van behind him.

Fat Tony leapt into his van and began **frantically** searching for more ammunition, but there was nothing left. He thrust his furious face out through the serving-hatch window. 'Now look what you did!' he **screamed** at Tony Two-scoops. 'All my hot dogs are gone!'

'Well, you jolly well got what you deserved!' Tony Two-scoops **yelled** back, throwing empty ice-cream tubs into the road.

Fat Tony had already started his engine, and roared away along the seafront, making rude hand gestures from his window and shouting, 'I'll be back!'

'So much for breakfast,' Tommy sighed as the vans disappeared in opposite directions.

'It's not really a very healthy breakfast anyway, is it?' Freddie frowned, stepping over the hot dogs scattered on the pavement.

'And that, my friend, is one of the few perks of being a ghost: there's no such thing as unhealthy when you're dead. Hot dogs for breakfast, lunch and tea. Come on, I think I've got a tin back at the Ghost Train.'

'Ugh,' Freddie replied, standing in a slop of melting ice cream as he tiptoed carefully through the remains of the food fight.

Back at the Town Hall, Mayor Jackson was trying to restore order in the Beach Suite. 'Ladies and gentlemen, please be quiet!' he shouted above the din. Noticing the crowd were now shouting at each other rather than at him, he decided to do what he did best in such situations: run away.

Stepping over his squished bowler hat of importance, he led Guy quietly from the noisy room into Marjory's office where he found his preferred headwear, a straw beach hat. Marjory was no longer sitting on her swivel chair, but instead was cowering behind it with her hands covering her face, watching her laptop through the gaps between her fingers. On the screen an elderly lady was describing how she had been attacked by a bowl of **GHOSTLY** spaghetti hoops.

'Just popping over to the funfair with Mr Walker, Marjory, to show him the **TUNNEL OF DOOM** and see if we can't come to some sort of arrangement with Mr McNasty,' said the Mayor.

Marjory's only response was a high-pitched squeak.

Spangles McNasty was as happy as a fish as he swung **Double Bad** through the funfair gates. 'No one ever **gave** me nothin' before, Sausage,' he said. '**Everything** I own, I had to **steal** myself,' he added proudly.

He suddenly wished he'd told his aunt Nugget this before she died, and he wanted to thank her for giving him such an amazing, huge, spangly—

Spangles' happy thoughts suddenly skidded to an abrupt halt along with **Double Bad** as he squeezed the bike's brakes in shock.

The **TUNNEL OF DOOM** was indeed amazing and huge. But it was also broken. And worst of all, as far as Spangles could see, it was made of wood.

'It's . . . it's . . . ' Spangles stammered.

'Brilliant!' Sausage said, looking up in absolute awe at the enormous roller coaster.

'That ain't quite the word I was looking for, Sausage.'

'Awesome?' Sausage suggested.

'**Wooden,**' Spangles corrected his friend, knocking on one of the many supporting pillars with a disappointed fist.

His eyes followed the track UP and over and round

and down

and up again and round

and round;

from start to finish, it
was all wooden.

'Not a spangle in
sight,' he mumbled sadly.
'What was she thinking?
What am I supposed to
do with this?'

'We could **re-open** it. It's an antique roller coaster – people would come from all over to ride it. **We'll be rich!**' Sausage answered in a rare moment of sensibleness.

Spangles considered this suggestion, gazing at his **inheritance**. The track was full of holes, the pillars were cracked, and the ticket office, control room and even the roller-coaster cars were made of **wood**. The only remotely **shiny** thing about the whole ride was the plastic sign, which looked new.

'**Better** name though: the **TUNNEL OF DOOM**,' Sausage said, reading the sign. 'Used to be "The Trundler" when we was **little**, do you remember?' Spangles remembered the old roller coaster with its old name of course, but had no idea his aunt had recently bought it and changed the name.

'Oh nuggets,' he sighed, like a deflating dream. 'Maybe she was going to repair it?'

'But the repairs would be costly and complex,' Sausage said, with an even rarer burst of intelligent vocabulary.

'And all kinds of boring,' Spangles complained. 'Like inventing golden tin foil.'

'We could sell it!' Sausage said. He had turned into an ideas factory. Not literally. He wasn't made of bricks and chimneys and conveyor belts, he'd just had three good ideas in less than a minute. That was three more than he'd had in the rest of his whole entire life.

'Whoa now,' Spangles said, amazed at Sausage's helpful outbursts. 'Are you feeling all right, Sausage? *We could sell it . . .*' he repeated slowly. Selling things was a totally new notion to Spangles, he had only ever stolen things before.

Then he frowned up at the antique roller coaster. 'But who would buy *that*?'

'I would,' a voice wearing an American accent offered.

Mayor Jackson stepped forward and introduced his new friend to his old enemy.

'Mr McNasty, Mr Sausage-face, may I introduce Guy Walker. Mr Walker is an antiques dealer. He specialises in antique roller coasters and has travelled all the way from America to see YOUR TUNNEL OF DOOM.'

'And to buy it,' Guy added confidently. 'And, please, call me Guy.'

'This guy wants to **buy** that?' Spangles repeated, astonished.

'I'll pay any price,' Guy offered. 'I simply must have it.'

'This guy will pay **any** price,' Spangles whispered to Sausage, trying his hardest to believe the words as he repeated them.

'In fact I'll pay **more** if you can get it working,' Guy continued. 'I'd like a test ride before I buy, gentlemen. Shall we say early this evening, nineteen hundred hours?'

'This guy wants to **try** it and **buy** it,' Spangles repeated in a hushed and confused whisper. 'Something about **hundreds** of hours?'

Most days were simple for Spangles McNasty; he ate cold **greasy** chips from bins, he **shouted** at babies, he pulled faces at old ladies, he **farted** in the library and he stole **spangly** things. But this particular day was being all kinds of **WEIRD**. 'Why would **anyone** want to buy a huge, broken, **unspangly** thing?' he wondered to himself.

'Something **smells** fishy, and I don't mean his **beard**,' he announced, jabbing a thumb into Sausage's fake whiskers and staring at Mayor Jackson and his American friend. He hoped that giving the situation the stare would somehow make it more understandable.

'Money talks,' Guy said, and turned to go.

'**About what?**' Sausage asked, and joined the staring.

'We'll see you this evening, gentlemen, for the test ride. Good day.' Mayor Jackson bid the two thieves a polite farewell and left with Guy.

'**Forget** the talking money. **Bring gold!**' Spangles shouted after them. He continued staring as they walked away into the funfair, but it didn't help.

He was as confused as a teabag, as no one ever says, but they should.

'I think there's more to this broken roller coaster than meets the eye, me old sledge-hammer. Why is that guy so keen to have it? And what does he talk to his money about?' Sausage said.

'Maybe Aunt Nugget left something else inside, something spangly. Let's take a closer look,' Spangles suggested hopefully, as he used his new key to unlock the ticket-office door.

Spooky

Freddie looked up and up and up at the **TUNNEL OF DOOM**. It was huge.

'Scary,' said Tommy the Ghost. 'But not as scary as this: **"WHOOOOOO".'** Freddie turned to see Tommy in the seat behind waving his arms above his head and saying

'WHOOOOOO'.

They had found a tin of hot dogs and were now riding **TOMMY'S GHOST TRAIN** before it opened for the day. The train had just emerged from the dark interior of the ride onto the sunny balcony. Freddie looked at **TOMMY THE GHOST** and shook his head. 'It's heights I'm **scared** of, Tommy. Not people who think they're ghosts hiding under bed sheets, going, **"WHOOOOO"**.'

Tommy switched off the engine. The train could be driven remotely from the control room by the ride's entrance, for **HAUNTING**, or manually, for fun.

He climbed out of the train. 'Come on, there's a good view of the roller coaster up here.' He motioned Freddie to follow him up a spiral staircase that led onto a roof.

Once there, Freddie tried looking up at the **TUNNEL OF DOOM** but it made him dizzy, so he tried looking down instead, but that was worse. Worse with an unexpected nasty bonus when he saw the familiar figures of **Spangles McNasty** and **Sausage-face Pete** unlocking the roller coaster's ticket-office door and stepping inside.

'Did you see that, Tommy? Those two thieves, **Spangles** and his sausage-faced friend, are down there. What are they up to?'

Before Tommy could reply, Freddie was already halfway down the spiral staircase, 'Just going to see what Mayor Jackson knows about this,' he shouted, relieved to be heading back to ground level.

Mayor Jackson **marched** back through the funfair more than a little worried. So **worried** in fact, he didn't even notice Wendy McKenzie

calling good morning to him as she opened her goldfish and candyfloss stalls for the day.

'Do you think he'll sell?' Guy asked as they left the funfair.

'Oh, he'll sell all right,' the Mayor replied, hiding his own doubts. 'He just needs a little extra persuasion, that's all.' He took out his phone and called Marjory.

Marjory was hiding in the stationery cupboard when the phone rang. The finale of SPOOKY COOKY had been particularly CREEPY. A bunch of carrots had mysteriously appeared in an elderly lady's fruit bowl, and then fruit started appearing in her cupboards amongst the cups and saucers. The lady admitted she was a little forgetful, but the presenter insisted her kitchen had become HAUNTED by the well-known Fruit-and-Veg Menace and the only solution was to blitz the lot up in a blender into a delicious smoothie. Which he then poured over the lady's head.

It was at this point that Marjory hid in the cupboard.

She peekcd through the keyhole at the ringing phone on her desk. *This is ridiculous*, she thought to herself in her cupboard. *There's no Fruit-and-Veg Menace here. There's not even a fruit bowl.* Taking a deep breath, she darted out of the cupboard, grabbed the phone and leapt back in, slamming the door closed. 'Hello,' she said shakily. 'Is there anybody there?'

'Marjory, take a telegram, would you?' Mayor Jackson ordered as he continued marching back to the Town Hall. Mayor Jackson was a little old-fashioned and liked to call emails telegrams and imagined they were delivered by horses. Not horses that could read of course, but horses with riders in smart uniforms with little hats.

'It's for all the funfair traders.

"Dear fun people, you may have heard a rumour this morning that a certain Spangles McNasty is back in town and that he is the new owner of the TUNNEL OF DOOM."

Well, he is actually, so it's not really a rumour, I suppose. Anyway . . . Marjory, are you typing this?' The phone line was silent.

'The poor woman, he poured it all over her head. A fruit-and-veg smoothie it was . . .' Marjory whispered, backing into the corner of her cupboard.

'Ermm. Okaaay . . . ' Mayor Jackson replied. 'Well, just let them know I'm dealing with it.'

'With the smoothie?'

'No, Marjory, with Spangles McNasty. There's nothing for anyone to worry about. He will soon be selling the TUNNEL OF DOOM and then he'll be gone. That's it. That's the message. Oh, and tell them there's a test ride this evening at seven o'clock.'

'It's *haunted*, you know, Mayor. HAUNTED,' Marjory replied.

'The **TUNNEL OF DOOM**?' The Mayor wondered what had got into his secretary lately and then suddenly, almost accidentally, he had a great idea. A fabulous idea in fact. He hung up the phone, ushered Guy Walker into a restaurant they were passing, suggesting a late breakfast, and then hurriedly dialled his nephew **TOMMY THE GHOST**.

Mayor Jackson had known Tommy since he was a baby, and was pretty certain he was alive and well and not even **SLIGHTLY DEAD**.

As far as he could remember, Tommy had got the idea he was a **GHOST** into his head from a **GHOSTLY** cartoon series he became obsessed with as a child. When he was old enough, little Tommy started working on his parents' **GHOST TRAIN** in Bitterly Funfair, taking over the whole operation when they retired to live in France. Tommy still insisted his parents had both died and were now working on a ghost train abroad, even though they often sent postcards and Mayor Jackson had been to visit them twice.

He had occasionally tried to explain this to Tommy but, just this once, he thought, what harm could it do to encourage his nephew's **GHOSTLY AMBITIONS?**

After a quick conversation about ghosts, roller coasters, hotels and hot dogs, Mayor Jackson convinced Tommy how much better the end of the pier would be once the **TUNNEL OF DOOM** was removed and replaced by his own latest and greatest tourist attraction, 'The Grande Splash Hotel' with its window water slides. It would mean more customers for the Ghost Train, and he'd even throw in a lot of hot dogs for Tommy's trouble. All Tommy had to do was haunt the TUNNEL OF DOOM and scare away Spangles McNasty and Sausage-face Pete.

Tommy was so pleased someone was finally taking his death seriously he would have agreed to almost anything, hot dogs or not.

Mayor Jackson congratulated himself on his excellent mayoring skills and joined Guy in the restaurant to celebrate.

Half an hour later Spangles and Sausage were slowly walking the track of the **TUNNEL OF DOOM**, taking care to step over the gaping holes and missing sections. They'd searched the office and control room but found no gold so far. 'You know them Americans from that America,' Spangles said. 'They have **loads of gold**. All of 'em.'

'All of 'em?' Sausage asked, unsure of this rather bold claim. 'Even the baby ones?'

'Yup,' Spangles continued. 'They had a **"Gold Rush"** once upon a time – you know, like history or fairy tales or something – and they found it in rivers like fish. Now there's so much they use it as pavements in New York village.'

They walked on in silence for a moment,

approaching the actual tunnel of the **TUNNEL OF DOOM**. 'So that guy . . . ' Sausage thought aloud.

'**Yup,**' Spangles answered. 'Bags of it, **me old golden nugget**. Loads of lovely **spangly** gold to buy this **old heap of junk**. Maybe that's what Aunt Nugget wanted me to do with it?'

As they stepped into the gloom of the tunnel together, Spangles started counting to a million pounds as that is how rich he thought he was about to become. Sausage couldn't stop thinking about talking money. What did it talk about? And to who? He was still thinking about this when **TOMMY THE GHOST** suddenly leapt out of the shadows screaming.

Tommy had never attempted haunting outside of his ghost train before, so he'd made an extra effort, wearing a glow-in-the-dark skeleton mask and a frizzy white wig he'd borrowed from one of the ghost train dummies.

He said as **SPOOKILY** as he could, 'I am the ghost of the **TUNNEL OF DOOOOOOOOM**! Get out of my tunnel, get out!' Then for good measure added the traditional,

'WHOOOOOOO!'

Sausage-face Pete jumped up onto Spangles, shrieking, 'Mummy!' Spangles caught him calmly and said, 'I don't think that's your mother, Sausage. I think it might be . . . It couldn't be . . . could it? Aunt Nugget, is that you?'

This was not quite the reaction Tommy the Ghost had been hoping for. On the Ghost Train people usually just screamed and then went home. They didn't ask questions.

He decided to play along, and replied, 'Yes, dear,' in his highest, squeakiest voice. 'I am the ghost of your aunt Nugget.'

'Erm. You look well,' Spangles said uncertainly.

'Thank you,' Tommy replied. 'Being a GHOST isn't so bad.'

She didn't sound like the aunt Spangles

remembered, but maybe a bit of **DEATH** changed people; he'd never met a ghost before, so he didn't really know. 'What should I do, Aunt Nugget? **Why** did you **give me** the **TUNNEL OF DOOM**?' he asked the strange figure who wouldn't stop leaping and flapping her arms.

'You were always a *good* boy, Spangles, you'll know what to do when the time is right,' Tommy replied with his best ghostly wisdom, followed by a long

'WHOOOOooo-ooooo-WHOOOOO'

Although this did in fact sound just like the sort of ghostly wisdom an actual for-real ghost might say, he probably should have got straight to the point and said; 'Sell this old roller coaster to Guy Walker **immediately** and leave Bitterly Bay for good,' which was what his uncle had told him to say.

But it was **already** too late.

Spangles McNasty's eyes widened and his caterpillar eyebrows began to dance. **'Of course!'** he yelled, dropping Sausage-face Pete on the tracks. **'Why** didn't I think of it **before?'**

'What?' Sausage and Tommy the Ghost said together.

'I'll do **exactly** what you taught me, Aunt Nugget – I'll **steal** that guy's gold!'

'Ah. Right, that . . .' Tommy said. 'Erm, well you could do that, or . . .'

Spangles had never hugged a ghost before, but he was so excited he decided now was the time to try. He ran towards Tommy the not-really-the-Ghost-of-Aunt-Nugget shouting, 'Give us a squeeze, auntie!' Tommy the not-really-any-sort-of-Ghost-at-all turned and ran into the darkness, screaming like he'd just seen a ghost himself.

Guaranteed to Make You Sick

Freddie had run out of the funfair gates and along the beach. He knew that the best place to find Mayor Jackson on a sunny day was at his beach-hut office. But he arrived to find a padlocked door with a sign hanging in the window reading:

Sorry, no one home today. For further assistance please call 4893271190 Your favourite Mayor W.T. Jackson ☺

Freddie took out his phone and dialled the number as he walked towards the promenade, weaving between a few early morning sandcastles.

The phone Freddie called was still in the stationery cupboard of Marjory's office with a very nervous Marjory. After ten rings and ten deep breaths she lifted the receiver and screamed, 'HELP!' which gave Freddie such a fright he dropped his phone. It landed with an unlucky splash in the moat of a rather ornate sandcastle.

With increasing panic, Marjory shouted repeatedly into the silent phone line:

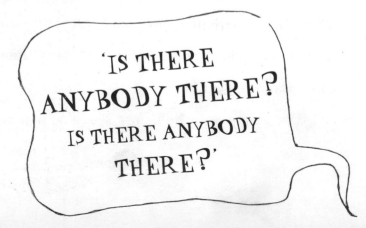

'IS THERE ANYBODY THERE? IS THERE ANYBODY THERE?'

Freddie fished his phone out of the water. It was completely dead. His mum wouldn't be happy about that, but he had more important things to worry about. So he ran all the way back to the funfair where he found Wendy McKenzie trying to decipher an email from Bitterly Town Hall.

'They're back, Wendy,' Freddie panted, arriving breathless at the goldfish stall. 'I've just seen Spangles McNasty and Sausage-face Pete at the TUNNEL OF DOOM. Have you heard anything?'

'Well, darling, funny you should ask. Take a look at this.' Wendy spun her laptop round to face Freddie. He read the Mayor's message about Spangles with alarm.

'There's no way he'll just sell it and leave.

And what's that bit about the town being on "Haunted Smoothie Alert"?'

Wendy spun her laptop back. 'Beats me, darling,' she said, 'but someone should probably stop Spangles from doing whatever nastiness he's planning on doing before he does it, don't you think? And that same someone should probably ride the re-opened roller coaster this evening and face their fear of heights once and for all.'

'Maybe that someone could use a little help? Especially with the high-up bit,' Freddie said hopefully.

'No can do, darling. You know I never close my stalls.' She smiled at Freddie, pointed towards the GHOST TRAIN and added, 'You and Tommy are going to have to sort this without me.'

Spangles had given up chasing the ghost of his aunt in the dark tunnel, assuming she'd vanished back to ghost-land or wherever she'd come from.

(In actual fact Tommy had run back to the safety of his ghost train and was eating another comforting tin of hot dogs.)

Spangles and Sausage pedalled **Double Bad** at top speed along the promenade to the Sloshy Sushi in the harbour and began gathering tools for roller-coaster repairs. Spangles knew if they were going to steal that guy's gold, they had to get him on the roller coaster for his test ride. And there was no way anyone could ride the TUNNEL OF DOOM in its current state.

Sausage had a surprisingly large number of tools for boat maintenance, which were now in a pile on deck. Everything from hammers to spanners, super glue to rubbish glue and step ladders to rope ladders. Spangles' eyebrows danced the flipping dance of the 'Oh flips, now what?' when he realised the pile of tools wasn't going to fit into **Double Bad**'s basket as they had planned.

'Let's sail the Sloshy Sushi over to the pier, Sausage,' he suggested, pausing his eyebrows mid-flip, 'That way we can take everything we need.'

'And we can have a sushi snack whenever we want!' Sausage replied excitedly, 'And. . .' he added as he started the engine, 'and we can combine our two business ventures and sell people sushi as they gets to ride the TUNNEL OF DOOM.'

'Team focus!' Spangles suddenly yelled at his friend, trying to get him to concentrate on stealing gold and stop going on about all kinds of boring.

It didn't work.

'The TUNNEL OF DOOM, guaranteed to make you sick!' Sausage shouted over the chunder of the engine. 'That's it! That's what that sign should say,' he said, giddily pointing at his half-painted restaurant sign. 'You make a new sign, me old paint brush, and I'll sail the boat, all the way to the golden times.'

Spangles could feel a Sausage sea shanty coming on, and when Sausage started singing there was no way of stopping him, no matter how much the team focused. Spangles reached for the paint brush. 'But then no more boring talk. Just hammers and stealing gold. OK?'

Sausage nodded in agreement and let rip:

Ohhhhh . . .
Hammers and spanners, dead fish and gold,
Hurrah! Hurrah!
Tunnels with ghosts and fish on toast.
Hurrah! Hurrah!
Spooky fresh sushi, dead fish from the seas,
Loopy the loop, no cooky, no peas.
That guy's got loads of gold to nick,
Come and ride the Tunnel of Dooooooooooom!
. . . Guaranteed to make you sick!

Spangles' eyebrows danced their approval and he
joined his friend in the chorus Sausage had written
especially for him.

Heeeee's aaassssss nasty as a pasty
gone past its sell-by date!
A fartin' in libraaaareeeeeees nut case!
He eats cold chips scooped out of a bin,
He pulls faces at old ladies for lookin' at him,
He shouts at babies on a whim,
He collects other people's spangly thiiiiiiiiiiiiings,
so they calls him . . .
    Spangles! McNasty!
        OH YEAH!

Freddie was surprised to find the Ghost Train closed, although the office door was unlocked.

'Tommy?' he shouted through the doorway as he stepped inside.

'I'm in here,' came a muffled reply from somewhere nearby. It sounded a bit like someone sitting in a small cupboard, talking with their mouth full. Freddie opened the cupboard door to find TOMMY THE GHOST sitting on an upturned waste-paper bin surrounded by empty tins of hot dogs.

'What are you doing in the cupboard, Tommy?' he asked.

'Eating hot dogs,' Tommy replied. 'And hiding.'

'Hiding from what?'

'The new neighbours. They're really odd. Especially the baldy one. He's going to steal someone's gold. He told me. Then he tried to squeeze me!'

'Spangles McNasty?' Freddie checked.

'Ughghhh,' Tommy replied, trembling at the memory of his close encounter.

'He's re-opening the **TUNNEL OF DOOM** tonight. It must be part of his plan. But how's he going to steal gold, Tommy, and from who?'

'Don't know, don't care.' Tommy replied. 'And no, I'm not going back, before you ask. No way,' he concluded, putting an end to his own involvement in any further **TUNNEL OF DOOM** adventures.

Tommy's refusal to help sounded pretty final. As a last resort Freddie tried the only thing he knew Tommy the Ghost couldn't resist.

'If you help me climb up to the tunnel, I'll buy you a hot-dog breakfast at Fat Tony's every day for the rest of the summer.'

Tommy leapt to his feet. 'Why didn't you say so earlier?! Let's go!'

After checking from the Ghost Train's roof that the coast was clear, they decided the easiest way up was to walk the roller-coaster's track backwards. Not walking backwards of course, but starting from the end of the track and walking back along it towards the start.

Like all roller coasters, the TUNNEL OF DOOM started with a super-steep slope where the coaster cars are slowly pulled up to the highest point of the track, then tipped over a ridge onto a madly sharp drop and a long ride back to ground level. The later stages of the track after the loop the loops were more and more gentle.

Some of the track had nice, safe wooden fencing around it, which Freddie liked the look of immediately, some was completely exposed and full of holes, which he was less keen on. After the final loop the loop, near the end of the ride was the tunnel itself.

Tommy had climbed straight up one of the supporting pillars earlier to do his haunting but knew it would be easier, especially for Freddie, to walk up the track. They agreed to hide in the tunnel and spy on Spangles, assuming he'd turn up sooner or later. In case it turned out to be later, Tommy insisted they each carry a heavy rucksack filled with tins of hot dogs.

They had walked about five metres and were a metre above ground level when Freddie froze.

'Slight problem,' he shouted ahead to Tommy. Tommy the Ghost turned and saw Freddie the Statue half crouched and perfectly still.

'Really?' Tommy said, incredulously. 'That's as far as you can go?'

He walked back to where Freddie was statue-ing, thinking over possible solutions to himself: 'Trampoline? Jet packs? Drive a car up? Drive a train up? Drive a train up! Genius!'

Tommy's ghost train was pulled around its spooky ride by a looks-a-bit-like-a-steam-train-but-powered-by-batteries little engine. The train was just about small enough for two people to pick up and carry from a ghost train to a roller coaster (luckily built for the same size track) and just about powerful enough to drive uphill. Very, very slowly.

A few minutes later, that's exactly what was happening.

'Doesn't it go any faster?' Freddie asked, his eyes shut tight again.

'Oh, you're a speed monster now, are you? A minute ago you were playing statues,' Tommy replied, as they crept onward and upward. The little engine had a built-in safety mechanism stopping it from going any faster, which Tommy thought was just as well because it gave him time to look out for any holes in the track as they climbed. So far, so good.

'Open your eyes and enjoy the view, Freddie, it's perfectly safe. Sort of,' he said. His own eyes were suddenly drawn across the bay to a particular boat leaving Bitterly Harbour with two strange figures dancing around what appeared to be a pile of old junk on deck.

He hoped it wasn't who he thought it probably was and turned away, willing the little train to go just a little bit faster.

The Fix

Sausage-face Pete tied **the Sloshy Sushi** to the pier directly beneath the **TUNNEL OF DOOM** and propped one of his many ladders against the pier's railings high above them. Spangles was half way up the ladder when the little **GHOST-TRAIN** engine finally dragged itself into the tunnel and safely out of sight.

After two more trips each up and down the

ladder, everything was piled messily in front of the roller coaster. 'Right then, Sausage, **to work!**' Spangles said, grinning the grin of the soon to be rich and rubbing his nasty collecting hands together.

'**Right then,**' Sausage repeated. 'Do you know much about structural engineerin', **me old tool belt**? Joinery? Masonry? Electricals? That sort of thing.'

'Not a **sausage**, Sausage. But I've got me own **hammer** – how hard can it be?' Spangles said as he marched towards the track to get started.

High above him, Freddie and Tommy had hidden the little ghost-train engine in a dark corner of the tunnel off the track. They were peeking through a hole in the rotting wooden wall. 'I can't hear what they're saying, Tommy. You'll have to get closer. We need to know how they're going to steal the gold,' Freddie said quietly.

'Me?' Tommy squeaked.

'I can't go – I'm scared of heights.'

'I'm not going anywhere near that loon.' Tommy shivered at the memory of his recent Spangles encounter.

'But you're already a ghost. What's the worst that could happen?'

The whispering argument continued and no one went anywhere.

Spangles quickly realised they were going to need a lot of wood to patch up the missing bits of track and even more quickly concluded he wasn't about to go and buy any as there was plenty right there under his feet.

'You mean the pier, don't you, me old lumber jack?' Sausage checked as they rummaged amongst the tool pile for the chain saws.

'Abso-choppin'-lutely. This bit 'ere is all mine anyway,' Spangles said, waving a hammer in the general direction of the end of the pier, 'so it ain't even stealin'. Which is a shame,' he added thoughtfully.

The chain-sawing, bashing and hammering began. Wood was taken from the pier surrounding and even underneath the roller coaster, chopped up and hammered into place to patch up the antique ride. Anything they didn't need or want they threw into the sea, including bits of track, a sofa from the office, a filing cabinet, a microwave oven and a family of mice living in an old shoe box stuffed with straw.

They stopped for a break around lunchtime and sat on one of the highest sections of track, swinging their naughty legs merrily in the midday sun. To Spangles' delight, Sausage fished a big blue tea pot and two red mugs from one of the unfeasibly large pockets of his yellow fisherman's mac and a plate of chocolate biscuits from the other. The tea pot had a cork in the spout and an elastic band over the top holding the lid on. 'A fisherman is always prepared, me **old tea break**,' he said, uncorking the pot.

'This is the life, eh, Sausage?' Spangles said with an excitable grin, 'Ain't nothin' in this world as smashin' as carefully prepared nastiness.'

'I'll **drink** to that,' Sausage said, and clunked mugs with Spangles, sloshing tea over his mac.

'To nasties!'

'And **gold!**' Spangles returned the clunk and sloshed more tea towards the ground far below.

'You do realise that guy wants to buy this old heap of junk, don't you, **me old shop keeper?**' Sausage said, 'Maybe we could just fix it up and sell it and get rich all proper, **no stealin'**, likes?'

'I 'ad been thinkin' about that, Sausage,' Spangles said, looking dreamily out to sea. 'Thing is though, what would Aunt Nugget think of me if I did that? **No stealin'**? And anyway, what if he don't like the test ride? Then he won't buy it an' he'll take all his lovely spangly gold back to the America. I reckons, we rob his gold and *then* if he still wants to buy it, we sell him this old heap of junk!'

'Ha ha! When you puts it like that, me old shops an' robbers, I reckon I agree,' Sausage said and raised his mug for another clunk.

'We should have a secret scarper signal, in case it all goes wrong,' Spangles said, his criminal mastermind on a roll.

'Like a silent fart?' Sausage suggested.

'Well, no. It would have to be a noise that anyone could hear, but only we knew it meant, Hush now and scarper quick 'n' quiet, likes.'

'Oh. Like a noisy fart?' Sausage offered.

'Maybe.' Spangles mulled it over as a seagull landed on the track a few feet away. 'Or a seagull squawk — that would be a good 'un.'

'Speakin' of plans, how do we do the actual stealin', then?' Sausage asked, looking along the track as it curved into the tunnel in the distance.

'We do it in there, I reckons.' Spangles gestured towards the tunnel with his mug of tea. 'We stop the coaster cars in the dark, make a lot of distracting noise, grab the gold and bish-bosh-hoo-har! We're rich!' It all seemed perfectly simple to Spangles.

Sausage-face Pete knew plenty about sailing, nothing at all about sushi restaurants, but surprisingly, he did know a little something about roller coasters. 'The tunnel can do the dark, I can do the distractin' with some of me singing and you can do the golden grab. But who starts and stops the ride? The startin' and stoppin' lever is down there' – Sausage pointed to a little wooden shack next to the ticket office – 'in the control room.'

'**Oh**. Don't we drive it round like a car, then?'
Spangles worried at the unexpected road block.

'Coooo-eeeee!' A voice drifted up from below.
'Coffee anyone?'

Vinegar Jones had tried to resume scowling at
her kettle after Spangles had left her café early that
morning but found she couldn't stop smiling.
She didn't know this particular facial expression
was called a smile as she had never done one
before. She had decided the strange stranger must
be responsible for this, and that she must find him
and tell him of the effect he'd had on her face.

Vinegar packed her clockwork coffee machine and favourite coffee beans – Badass Bitter Roast – which were famously grown by the bitterest farmer in the world: **Old Farmer Angrypants**, who swore bitterly at his crops all day and watered them with his own tears.

A quick chat with her neighbour, Mrs Tinker from Tinker's Trinkets Gift Shop, had revealed the stranger with the tin-foil hat, tie and moustache combination was the man who had just inherited the **TUNNEL OF DOOM**.

And the new owner of the **TUNNEL OF DOOM** was the talk of the town, so tracking him down was a piece of cake. Not that Vinegar liked cake. The only thing she'd ever liked was coffee. She'd always had a funny feeling about it, and now she was feeling the same funny feelings for Spangles McNasty; she didn't know why, but she liked it.

She flipped the sign on the door of her café over, from 'We're open – go away!' to 'We're closed – get lost!', unchained her moped from the lamp post outside and rode along the beach, her scarf flapping merrily behind her as she bounced over children's sandcastles, laughing.

'We've got tea, **thanks**,' Sausage shouted down politely to the strange woman offering coffee from far below.

'Not you, stupid!' Vinegar shouted back, not quite so politely. 'I was talking to the handsome gentleman sitting next to you.'

Spangles and Sausage looked around for a handsome gentleman, but there was no one else there. 'He's not in,' Spangles replied. 'Get off **my property.** No loons **allowed**.'

Oh, how she liked him when he was rude.

Vinegar Jones giggled and produced a bunch of flowers from behind her back. She held them up towards the man that made her face do the weird thing.

In return, Spangles casually emptied the remains of his tea in her direction. Vinegar sidestepped the incoming tea and blushed. She hearted him completely, with all her beans. As the beginning of a budding romance, this may seem a little odd, but to Vinegar Jones, it was perfect.

'I've written a poem!' she shouted.

'Who is this nutter?' Spangles asked Sausage.

'That's Vinegar Jones from the weird coffee shop on the promenade. Proper potty, she is.'

'Can I read you my poem . . . Spangles?' Vinegar giggled at the sound of his name.

'She seems to know you,' Sausage teased.

Vinegar began reciting her poem from memory:

Coffee is bitter, violets are blue,
Tea is rubbish, and I heart you.
Oh Spangles McNasty,
so very, very rude.
McNasty, McNasty,
I would do anything for you.

'That last bit doesn't really rhyme properly yet. I was in a hurry. Sorry.'

'Doesn't rhyme at all,' Sausage said to Spangles. 'She is soooo weird.'

Spangles' collecting mind cogs were too busy removing road blocks to notice Sausage's comment.

'Did you say you'd do "anything"?' he shouted to Vinegar.

Twenty minutes and a good deal of giggling later, Vinegar Jones was **prodding** the roller coaster's controls like a professional. Spangles had explained that they needed someone to start and stop the coaster cars during the **test** ride that evening. There was no need to tell her any more than that.

The **naughties** thanked Vinegar for her help and coffee, and finally waved her on her way.

'Until tonight you naughty, **naughty** man,' she said, still smiling the biggest smile of her life.

Spangles did his best grin and waved until his arm ached and the **loopy lady** was out of sight. 'She is **soooo weird**,' he said at last, rubbing his aching arm and staring after the **strange** lady.

There was something odd about her, something he couldn't understand and it was giving him the hoo-bee-jim-jams big time.

'Still, that **solves** that little **problemo**,' he said, snapping out of his ponderings. 'Now **all** we have to do is **finish** the repairs before seven o'clock this evening.' He looked up at the track; they were less than a quarter of the way along when they'd stopped for tea. 'It's gonna be a **long** day, Sausage, but it'll be **worth** it. This time tomorrow . . . we'll be **stinkin' rich**.'

The sun shone down on this unusual scene. Although it was quite possibly the oldest and wisest celestial body in the complete COSMOS, having had more than four and a half billion birthdays, it *still* didn't know what Spangles was up to and couldn't take its rays off him.

Freddie and Tommy had overheard Vinegar's poem too from their tunnel hideaway and were equally puzzled. 'What was all that about?' Tommy asked.

'I think that was Vinegar Jones from the little café on the promenade. Looks like Spangles has got himself an admirer.' Freddie shook his head at this latest unexpected turn of events.

Bish-Bosh-Hoo-Har

In the middle of the afternoon, Spangles and Sausage hung a tarpaulin sheet over either end of the tunnel, making it so dark they didn't see the little ghost-train engine or Freddie and Tommy hiding behind it. They just walked through, nailing a few extra planks of wood over the holes in the tunnel walls as they went.

Freddie waited ten long dark minutes after

they'd left, then shuffled up to the tarpaulin sheet and pulled it sideways slightly, letting light seep back into the tunnel.

'If they want it dark, maybe they're planning on doing something in here,' he said.

'Or they might just want to scare the riders. Parts of my ghost train ride are pitch black,' Tommy suggested.

TOMMY THE GHOST was so SCARED that Spangles might re-appear and hug him he spent the whole day hiding behind the engine playing games on his phone until the battery ran out, while Freddie spent most of the afternoon peeking through a crack at the gathering crowd below.

'They're putting a new sign up over the entrance.

It says, "The **TUNNEL OF DOOM**, guaranteed to make you sick!"' he said. 'And there's a long table with plates and a table cloth and some buckets . . . Those two are soooo weird.'

Spangles and Sausage had worked non-stop since their tea break, patching up the antique, unspangly ride.

The track was once again whole rather than full of holes. They were tired but giddy with collecting excitement. Three large Badass Bitter Roasts each had woken them up nicely. They were delivered by an equally excitable Vinegar Jones, who arrived on time and on her moped.

She was now locked safely inside the control room with her start-stop-start instructions and her **wildly** beating heart.

Spangles felt relieved she was safely behind a locked door but at the same time, he **really** wanted to go back for another coffee.

'**Anyone for sushi?**' Sausage asked the crowd at exactly seven o'clock. He couldn't understand why they were all standing so far back and holding their noses.

The crowd parted like an old-fashioned haircut as Mayor Jackson and Guy Walker arrived. Mayor Jackson had tried phoning his nephew Tommy the Ghost earlier to see if the haunting had been successful, but couldn't get through, so he assumed not and was now really, really hoping Spangles would just sell the TUNNEL OF DOOM anyway.

'Good evening, gentlemen,' he said, extending his hand for a shake of importance.

Sausage mistook the handshake of importance for a hand in need of sushi and immediately scooped a large slosh of rotten dead fish from one of his buckets onto a paper plate and handed it to the Mayor. The thin paper plate was no match for the heavy fish slop and salty sea water.

136

It promptly collapsed, spilling the stinky mess all over the Mayor.

'Gentlemen,' he said, calmly brushing slimy fish heads off his suit, as only the most patient of Mayors could, 'are we ready for our test ride?'

'We **certainly** is,' Spangles answered, feeling genuinely pleased with himself. 'If that guy could just follow me an' my **accomplice**— I mean, my **assistant**.' He gave Vinegar Jones a thumbs-up to signal that the game was on.

Guy Walker climbed into the front seat of the first roller-coaster car with some difficulty. He took off his hat and sat with his long legs folded neatly in half, his chin almost resting on his knees. Mayor Jackson was about to climb in next to him when Spangles stopped him. 'Now, now, Mayor – it ain't you buyin' so it ain't you ridin'.'

Mayor Jackson was about to argue, but changed his mind when he realised exactly what Spangles had just said. Perhaps he was planning on selling the **TUNNEL OF DOOM** after all.

Spangles climbed into the seat behind Guy, who was so squished he barely had room for the large bag he was carrying. 'Would you like me to look after your bag, Guy?' the Mayor asked.

'That won't be necessary,' Spangles snapped, guessing exactly what was inside the bag.

Lovely, spangly gold.

If it was full of talking money, he'd have heard it by now, but it hadn't said a word.

'Just pop it there, see, we can strap it in.' Spangles leant across and fastened the seatbelt over the bag on the seat next to Guy.

'Better for weight distribution, me old seesaw,' Sausage added, heaving a bucket of dead fish slop onto his seat next to Spangles.

'What on Earth are you doing, Sausage?'

Spangles hissed, glaring at his collecting accomplice.

'I ain't leavin' all this sushi behind – they'll nick it,' Sausage whispered back, dragging the second bucket on board.

The roller coaster lurched forward as Vinegar Jones pulled the starting lever down from the STOP position, written in big shouty red capital letters, to GO, written in matching big green shouters.

Guy Walker gripped the safety rail in front of him with one hand and the handle of his bag with the other.

Inside the tunnel, Freddie joined Tommy hiding behind the little ghost-train engine. They listened nervously to the roller coaster slowly clanking its way to the top of the ride.

There was a short, quiet pause as it rolled over the track's peak, followed by a growing thunderous roar and three distinct screams as it careered down the other side.

Freddie and Tommy felt the tunnel vibrate with the approaching force. Spangles, Sausage and Guy felt the whole track wobble wildly from side to side beneath them and the crowd of spectators felt the pier suddenly begin trembling under their feet.

Freddie thought the two **naughties** would stop the ride in the tunnel and do mischief where no one could see them.

Spangles thought he was about to become rich. He was also thinking about Vinegar Jones but he didn't really know why.

TOMMY THE GHOST thought he was a ghost.

Sausage-face Pete was thinking maybe he needed **stronger** plates for his sushi.

Most of the crowd were thinking, **THE TUNNEL OF DOOM** *is so awesome it is making me tremble even when I am not on it,* and the rest of them were thinking, **THE TUNNEL OF DOOM** *is going to fall into the sea.*

Vinegar Jones was watching the ride closely and thinking about the funny rude man with his hat and his tallness and the funny way he talked all talky-talk-talk like that. *Oooooh*, she thought again. When the coaster cars disappeared into the tunnel, flapping through the makeshift curtain, she pushed the lever back up to the STOP position and began to count to thirty, just like Spangles had instructed.

As the ride slowed quickly to a halt inside the almost darkness of the tunnel, Spangles started counting too and Sausage started singing:

Ohhhhh . . . coasters and toasters and sushi for tea.

Hurrah! Hurrah!

Wave your hands in the air in the Tunnel of Doom.

Hurrah! Hurrah!

Did you like that last bit – the loop the loop,

With your hands in the air it's better than soup.

You don't need to hold on, cos your seatbelt's all strong,

Wave your hands in the air, with this subliminal

messaging song!

Half of the tunnel was in complete darkness but half was **dimly** lit by sunlight seeping in through the open curtain. Noticing it wasn't quite dark enough to hide the golden grab, Spangles added a few words of his own to the song:

And close your eyes! ♪ ♪ ♫
Close all of your eyes, for the thrill of the ride! ♩♩

Sausage nodded his approval of this almost rhyming, completely out of rhythm attempt at singing in the almost dark.

Guy Walker was a happy man. The **TUNNEL OF DOOM** was in working order, a little wobbly, but nothing that couldn't be repaired more effectively by his people back home. He let go of the safety rail and the bag, waved his hands in the air and closed his eyes, ready to *enjoy* the ride down.

Quick as a wink, Spangles *grabbed* Guy's bag, slipped it out of its seatbelt and passed it to Sausage, who stuffed it inside his yellow mac. The ride lurched forward as Vinegar Jones completed her counting, 'Twenty-eight . . . twenty-nine . . . thirty!' and pulled the lever back down to GO.

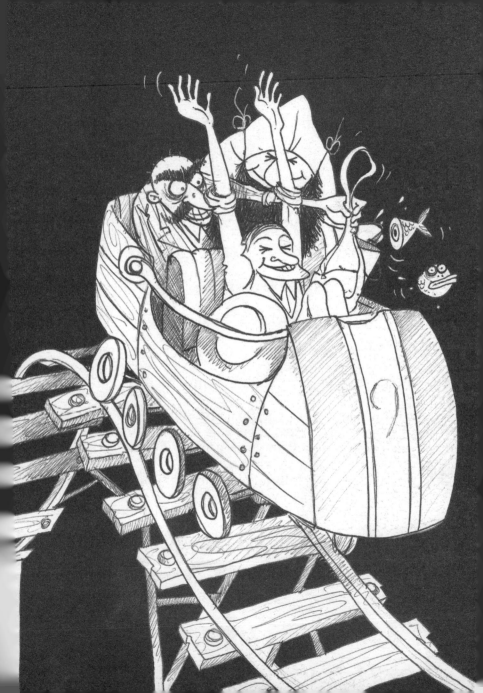

The coaster cars rolled out of the tunnel into the bright sunlight and charged down the next slope.

As soon as it was out of sight Freddie and Tommy leapt out from behind the ghost-train engine. 'Did you see that?' Freddie blurted excitedly. 'They stole that guy's bag. We need to get down there quickly and tell him.'

They heaved the ghost-train engine onto the track and climbed in. Tommy turned the key and it trundled slowly forward, almost as fast as a tortoise giving an elephant a piggy back.

'Can't this thing go *any* faster?' Freddie complained as it left the tunnel and rolled down the steep slope but surprisingly kept moving at the same sluggish speed. 'Not even downhill?'

'Nope. Safety first,' Tommy replied proudly. Freddie tried waving and shouting to the crowd below but it was hopeless – they were too far away and the noise of the wobbling track easily drowned out his cries for help.

It was all over too soon for Guy Walker. 'Again, again!' he demanded as soon as the roller coaster stopped at the end of the ride.

Spangles and Sausage leapt from their seat behind Guy and dived into the ticket office next to the control room, slamming the door shut behind them. 'Let's see the spangles on this!' Spangles declared, as giddy as a kipper. He yanked the bag open, only to have his spangly dreams flopped under the duvet of gloom for the second time in the same day.

'What's this?' he stammered.

'Ain't gold, that's what it is,' Sausage said, not exactly helpfully.

Spangles grabbed a fistful of American dollars from the bag and examined it closely.

'Funny money!' Sausage shrieked, poking it inquisitively to see if it would talk. 'What are we supposed to do with this? Where's the gold?' he asked the cash. 'You better start talkin' or we'll crumple you up.'

'Wait, wait, we don't need it to *talk*, Sausage! I think it's that American money, Billy Dollars, they calls it. All we 'ave to do is sail your boat to the America and swap it for gold from the pavements in New York village.'

'You're off the hook, funny money.' Sausage grabbed a handful of dollars himself and sniffed it before stuffing it under his hat in case it fancied a chat later.

'To the America!' Spangles declared, putting the rest of the cash back in the bag and helping Sausage hide it inside his mac.

They stepped triumphantly back outside into the sunshine and also into a right old rumpus. Mayor Jackson had noticed Guy's bag was missing and assumed the worst. Guy on the other hand was so excited about buying the old roller coaster he didn't really care about his missing bag. He just assumed he'd lost it and it would turn up again sooner or later. He had so much money he occasionally lost the odd pile, but he always found it eventually.

'What have you done with Mr Walker's bag?' Mayor Jackson demanded as Spangles and Sausage reappeared.

'Now, Mayor, it's no problem, really. I'm sure Mr McNasty had nothing to do with it.' Guy jumped to defend Spangles' honour and innocence. Something that had never happened before.

'I'm **innocent!**' Spangles declared, thinking this might turn into the happiest day of his entire nasty life. 'And now, my accomplice— I mean, my assistant and I must leave. **Goodbye,**' he added, deciding to leave with his honour intact and his bag of money in Sausage's mac.

'But I haven't paid you for the roller coaster yet?' Guy reminded him.

Spangles was marching towards Sausage's boat but stopped suddenly mid-stride, causing Sausage to walk straight into him. '**Oh**. I see. No, I suppose you haven't. Would you **still** like to?'

'Of course, of course. I can just go to the bank and get more money. It's no problem, really. No problem at all,' Guy offered happily.

Spangles had two confusing thoughts at once. Firstly: 'We already have a bag of **funny** money, we could run away now and live happily ever after!' And secondly: 'That guy wants to give me even more money and I don't even need to steal it this time!'

'Could you pay in gold please?' Spangles said. 'I prefers **gold**.'

'Sure, no problem. I'll go get it now, and then we'll have another ride, on *my* antique roller coaster, OK?'

'I'll just confer with my accomplice— I mean, my assistant,' Spangles said, turning his back on the crowd and whispering to Sausage, 'He gets the gold, he gives us the gold, we leave with the funny money and the gold. **Agreed**?'

Sausage thought for a moment, which was an unusually long time for him, and said, 'Or, he gets the gold, he rides again, we **steals** the gold, he gets even more gold, he rides again, we steals the **gold** . . . ' Sausage was trying to whisper but the thought of infinite gold was making him as **giddy** as infinite kippers.

Spangles grabbed him by his yellow collar and hissed, 'Hush your jibber-jabber there, Sausage! How about, he gets the gold, he rides again, we steals the gold, he gets even more gold, we sell the old heap of junk and we go to the America with one bag of funny money and two heaps of gold? **OK**?'

'Agreed, but if we're hanging around 'ere another second we need to stash the cash, **me old fruit machine**. What if it starts talking? He'll hear it.' Sausage was worried. 'People can **smell** money and greed and fear, but not as much as they can **smell** fish. I'll hide it in a sushi bucket.'

Spangles strode over to shake Guy's hand while Sausage stashed the cash in one of his buckets of fish stink in the coaster car.

The successful theft had put Spangles in such a good mood, he shouted, '**Free** rides for everyone!'

'**Free** sushi for all!' Sausage offered, overwhelmed with **fishy** generosity.

'No. Leave the sushi alone!' Spangles shouted, glaring at Sausage and hoping his face was conveying the rest of his unspoken message: *The stolen bag of talking money is in one of the sushi buckets.*

We don't want them to find the money, do we, Sausage?
No we don't.

Surprisingly, somehow Sausage understood perfectly.

'No more sushi for anyone. It's gone off,' he said. 'Stop those thieves!' Freddie shouted, as he and Tommy finally snailed it to the end of the ride.

Hurrah for Spangles and his Sausage-Faced Friend

Freddie hurriedly pushed his way through the crowd shouting, 'Spangles McNasty stole that man's bag in the tunnel!'

'No way!' the crowd shouted back as one. 'He seems a decent sort and he's just given us all a free go on his roller coaster. Hurrah for Spangles McNasty!' Considering this unanimous shout was completely unrehearsed, it was nothing short of a miracle that the whole crowd shouted the exact same words at the same time.

'Hurrah for Spangles McNasty and his sausage-faced friend!' the crowd continued in miraculous synchronised excitement and those with hats threw them in the air.

No one had ever **cheered** for Sausage-face Pete before. He found himself somewhat overcome with emotion, and before he had time to think he also found himself throwing his own hat (and beard attachment) in the air.

'**Oops**,' he said, as the dollars he'd stuffed inside it spilled all over Guy and Guy started yelling,

'Hey, that's my money! They really did steal my bag!'

Spangles decided to make a run for it. He dragged Sausage towards the roller coaster as he grabbed his flying hat by the beard and put them back where they belonged.

The coaster cars were already full of eager free riders. Spangles and Sausage quickly squeezed onto two seats with the two buckets of fish slop and hidden stolen cash and gave Vinegar Jones the double thumbs-up sign again. The ride immediately began clanking its way back up the starting slope.

As escape plans go, it was rubbish.

Worse than rubbish, but Spangles had panicked. They were on a roller coaster that could only go round in circles. As Spangles realised this, they clattered over the brow of the hill and roared down the other side. The whole structure shook more violently than before under the extra weight of the new passengers.

'Don't worry, Mayor, we'll get the money back!' Freddie shouted confidently as he and Tommy leapt back into their ghost-train engine. Tommy turned the key in the ignition and they trundled forward, like a sulky slug in a slug-and-rocket race.

'Well, this is awkward,' Freddie said to Tommy quietly as they rolled slowly past the Mayor and Guy Walker.

Guy frowned the frown that most visitors to Bitterly Bay frown sooner or later. 'This place is so weird,' he said to the Mayor, as the little engine crept up the starting slope slower than a sunrise.

'We need to go faster!' Freddie shouted, kicking the safety lever in frustration.

'What are you doing?' Tommy shrieked too late, as the lever snapped off. They suddenly started accelerating. 'There's a reason these engines have safety mechanisms built in.'

'Can you stop it?' Freddie asked, suddenly worried.

'I don't know, it's always had a safety lever before!' Tommy replied, as the little engine shot up the slope at an increasingly alarming rate.

The roller-coaster cars pulled into the tunnel and stopped. 'Why have we stopped?' someone asked from behind.

'Because you're a **monkey's bum!**' Spangles snapped, instantly ending his short-lived popularity.

'A monkey's red bum!' Sausage added, closing their new-found fan club for good.

The thirty-second stop inside the tunnel was almost enough for the speeding ghost-train engine to catch up. But not quite. Vinegar Jones pulled the control lever back down to GO, the coaster began its final descent and they were soon hurtling into the final bend.

'When we stops, **leg it!**' Spangles shouted his complicated escape plan over the roller's rattling racket.

'Where to, **me old runaway?**' Sausage asked.

'To the America, of course.'

'Isn't that a long way to run in **yellow wellies** with a **bucket full of sushi** hiding a bag of talking money?'

Spangles was about to add the words, 'On your boat!' and possibly, 'You massive idiot', when he was interrupted by an **explosive** cracking noise up ahead.

The badly repaired antique wooden track could take no more. The final bend **burst**, throwing bits of track in **all** directions and a shower of wooden splinters over Spangles and Sausage.

The section of pier beneath the roller coaster had also had quite enough of this nonsense, thank you very much. It gave one last sorrowful groan,

made a snap decision and went for a swim instead.

As the pier parts splashed into the sea, the broken track above seesawed wildly, pushing the snapped section up into the air.

A split second later the coaster shot off the end.

Freddie and Tommy had no way of stopping their **speeding** engine. They hurtled off the end of the broken track after the airborne coaster cars and flew over the funfair.

Freddie was too **terrified** to speak. He

thought he and Tommy the Ghost were about to become actual **FOR-REAL GHOSTS**.

Spangles thought they would probably, and conveniently, land on Sausage's boat and sail away to the America and be rich.

Sausage thought he would spill his sushi.

All of the excited fun-seeking free riders thought, *Wow, this is the best roller coaster we have ever been on!*

They were all wrong.

The coaster cars crash-landed onto the balcony of the **GHOST TRAIN** with an almighty clang, clatter and boom and a huge pile of luck. Their wheels touched down on the ghostly rails and, finding them to be just the right size, whizzed into the spooky darkness of the ride. Freddie and Tommy followed a split second later with an equally lucky, noisy landing of their own.

Sausage-face Pete started screaming and couldn't stop.

Spangles McNasty started laughing and couldn't stop.

All of the free riders started being completely silent and couldn't stop.

Freddie and Tommy just couldn't stop.

'What are you laughing at, me old giggle box?' Sausage asked between screams.

'I just can't believe we got away with it, is all, Sausage. Not only is we still alive, we've still got the funny money. We're rich! Why are you screaming?' Spangles asked between giggles.

'Because I spilt some of my sushi,' Sausage

170

replied, calming down a little and wrestling the bucket lids back into place.

'**Oh**, I thought it were because we landed in the Ghost Train.'

'In the what!?' Sausage said and started screaming all over again.

The Ghost Train was a tiny ride compared to the **TUNNEL OF DOOM** and the bends in its little track were much tighter. Mostly too tight, in fact, as they were all about to discover.

The coaster cars tried to follow the track round a sharp left bend and crunched to a sudden halt, sploshing more of Sausage's sushi over his wellies.

Silence fell in the darkness like a snowflake in a library.

Nobody moved.

The silent fun-seekers were all nervously wondering why they were sitting in darkness surrounded by gravestones, skeletons and ghostly figures when Freddie and Tommy collided with the back of the last jammed coaster car, finally stopping their little engine. 'Stop those thieves!' Freddie shouted.

'Oh flips,' Spangles said, suddenly serious. 'Where's the funny money, Sausage?'

Sausage splashed a hand into one of the stinky buckets, saying, 'In one of these 'ere buckets.'

'There's no time for that. Bring 'em both, quick, this way.' Spangles heaved one of the buckets of stink and possible riches and staggered off into the darkness.

'After them!' Freddie yelled,

clambering from the crashed little engine only to find his way completely blocked by the jammed coaster.

'We can cut them off this way.' Tommy pointed in the opposite direction and grabbed a mask, a wig and two sheets from a couple of nearby ghosty dummies as they ran.

Tommy put his haunting costume on and helped Freddie into his. They waited by a door in the darkness, listening carefully. 'OK. Here they come. When I open this door, leap through, wave your arms around and scream.

I'll do the rest,' he said.

They both leapt and screamed.

But not as loud as Sausage-face Pete.

'Aunt Nugget!' Spangles yelled in surprise.

Tommy had planned to tell the two thieves to give back the stolen bag or he'd haunt them for the rest of their naughty lives, but the sight of Spangles McNasty grinning madly quickly convinced him it had been a terrible idea and maybe he should run away again instead. So he did, closely followed by Spangles shouting, 'Just a **quick squeeze**, Auntie!'

Terrified, Sausage-face Pete followed. Freddie leapt around shouting **'WHOOOOO!'** on his own for a few seconds until he realised everyone else had gone. He stopped leaping and set off running after them.

Two quick corners, one staircase and one door later, Tommy the Ghost burst back into the sunlight of the pier and was welcomed by a slap in the face from a flying hot dog and a splat on the back of the head from a strawberry ice-cream cone.

Spangles, Sausage and Freddie ran out moments later to join him in the middle of Fat Tony and Tony Two-scoops' evening food fight.

'I say, old bean, now look what you've done,' Two-scoops said, reaching for the chocolate sauce.

'Sorry, Tommy' – Fat Tony apologised to his best customer, and continued throwing his slippery missiles –

'But you are sort of in the way!'

'Do move over, old sport,' Two-scoops suggested, squirting chocolate sauce all over everyone.

Tommy pulled off his ghosty disguise and, trying to get out of the way, ran backwards into Spangles McNasty.

Spangles gasped at the unveiling of the not-Aunt-Nugget-ghost and accidentally caught a hot dog in his gaping mouth. Fat Tony reached for the tomato sauce, extra jumbo economy size, so big he needed both hands to lift it. Freddie yanked his own ghosty sheet off over his head and at the same time slipped on a choc ice. He crashed into Sausage-face Pete, who slid into Tommy just as Fat Tony squeezed.

The sight of the coaster cars leaving the track had caused a sudden emotional panic in the heart of Vinegar Jones. She watched in horror as the loop the loops toppled like dominos, flattening the entire roller coaster ride. The only piece of the **TUNNEL OF DOOM** still standing was the control room she was sitting in and even that only had one wall left.

When Fat Tony **squirted** tomato sauce all over Spangles McNasty, she saw red.

She leapt into the **chaos** and grabbed Spangles by the bucket handle. 'Come with me, saucy,' she giggled, dragging him away from the carnage towards her moped. 'I know just the place we can hide.'

'Wait for Sausage, **me old rom com!**' Sausage pleaded, stepping over both Tommy the Ghost and Freddie, who were having difficulty getting up from the slippery floor.

'Not you, Mr Stinky-fish,' Vinegar snarled at Sausage as she helped Spangles onto the moped with his bucket.

'Well I ain't goin' **without** him, missus! And you did say anything?' Spangles reminded Vinegar.

Tommy and Freddie were still slipping over each other under the barrage of ice-cream and hot-dog missiles when Mayor Jackson arrived with Guy, just in time to see Vinegar's overloaded moped speeding away along the pier.

Freddie immediately started running after the escaping naughties, closely followed by Tommy.

'Say, isn't that the crazy lady from the coffee shop?' Guy Walker said, squinting into the setting sun, as he and the Mayor tried to keep up.

Kissy Kissy Fish Face

Vinegar Jones raced along the promenade and skidded to a halt in front of her café. They clambered off the moped and hurried inside.

'Quick, over here, you naughty man.' Vinegar ushered Spangles behind the counter and pointed to the four sacks of coffee beans beneath.

'This ain't no time for a **tasty sesh**, woman,' Spangles snapped, the panic rising in him like a volcano in a lift.

'No, silly. Climb in here with me, Spangles McNasty. Mr Stinky-fish, you hide in the huge shop-front window over there,' Vinegar explained.

'Maybe I'll hide in the window too – it's big enough for both of us,' Spangles said and tried to get away from Vinegar, but she had him by the bucket handle and wasn't about to let go.

'No, silly. You'll be seen straight away in the window, won't you?' Vinegar whispered. 'Let them catch their fishy man, while we hide in this sack,' she said with added blushing, giggling and winks.

Sausage-face Pete was already standing on the windowsill looking out into the street.

'I ain't sure this is the best hidin' place,' he said, suddenly spotting Freddie and Tommy running up the promenade. 'They're coming!' he shouted, leaping off the windowsill and then over the counter. 'Quick, in the sacks.' Without wasting another second arguing with the loopy lady, Sausage scrunched a welly into the nearest sack, squished his second in with it and started wriggling down, spilling coffee beans all over the floor.

Spangles quickly plunged his foot into the nearest sack, with Vinegar Jones still clinging on to the bucket handle. '**Listen**, missus, there ain't no way you're fittin' in 'ere anyhow. Let go of me **bucket.**'

'I'll let go of the bucket if you give me a kiss,' Vinegar replied with the biggest smile she had ever done.

Spangles looked around desperately for help. Sausage was almost completely submerged, only the top of his yellow hat and the bucket he was now holding above his head were still visible.

The situation was becoming hopeless. With his free hand, Spangles took Sausage's bucket and began shoving it into the coffee sack between them. 'Close your **eyes** then,' he said to Vinegar, not sure what to do next. The loose lid on Sausage's bucket slipped open again, and a moment of genius popped its ugly dead fish head out.

Spangles checked Vinegar Jones had her eyes shut, carefully and quietly lifted a stinky fish head from the bucket, and pressed its fishy face against Vinegar's cheek, making a kissy noise as he did so. Vinegar instantly let go of his bucket handle and collapsed in a fit of giggles.

Spangles quickly put the fish head back in Sausage's bucket, then shoved it deeper into the coffee sack and heaved his own in on top of it. Once it was completely submerged he wriggled himself down into his sack.

Vinegar suddenly stopped giggling, stood up, saw that everyone was hiding, and climbed into the fourth sack herself. She had just disappeared from view when Freddie and Tommy burst in through the café door.

It didn't take them long to search the small café – just long enough for Mayor Jackson and Guy to catch up.

Guy walked briskly behind the counter and saw the coffee-bean spillage. 'I called into this café earlier and the crazy lady hid under here.' He dragged the four heavy coffee sacks out of the way. 'Hmm. I guess not,' he said, satisfied there was no one under the counter.

Freddie led the way into the kitchen, which was separated from the café itself by a short corridor.

Spangles waited for the sound of footsteps to fade completely before slowly poking his baldy head up from his sack. He looked to his left, where the sack containing the buckets should have been then realised all the sacks had been moved. He quietly stood up and wriggled himself free.

Spangles looked at the other three identical sacks. One was full of dead fish and funny money, one was hiding his fishy friend and the third: *she* was in that one. It occurred to him that this would make a great TV game show: a lucky dip with one amazing prize, one pretty good prize and one . . . well . . . he wasn't sure what to think about the third prize, but she was definitely complicating things too much. He had to escape immediately *with* the funny money and *without* her.

He was trying to remember the *Hush now and*

scarper quick 'n' quiet signal they'd agreed on earlier when a seagull squawked loudly outside and suddenly Sausage-face Pete poked his head from the middle of the three sacks, holding the finger of hush to his lips.

Sausage quickly climbed free, leaving only one small problem. The two naughties looked at the two remaining sacks, one of which they definitely did want and one they definitely did not. Then they looked towards the kitchen, where the clattering noise of the search had suddenly stopped.

Spangles' caterpillar eyebrows panicked and tried to escape up his forehead and over his head. Sausage raised a finger skywards and grinned, signalling he'd had an absolute sausage of an

idea. Spangles urgently tapped his wrist where his watch would have been if he had one in that universally recognised gesture meaning, *Flippity flip-flops, hurry up!*

Sausage leant nose-touchingly close to the first sack, pulled his bushy beard aside and inhaled deeply, sniffing for the beautiful aroma of long-dead rotten fishies amongst the bitter smell of coffee. Mostly the first sack seemed to smell of coffee. He moved to the second sack to do the same.

Impatiently, Spangles give him an encouraging shove and squished his beardy face amongst the beans. Sausage gave the second sack the sniff and got a nose full of fish stink. Satisfied the second sack was proper fishy, thusly and therefore containing the buckets of fishies and the bag of funny money, Sausage stood and triumphantly pointed at it silently with both thumbs up.

As the sound of returning footsteps echoed along the corridor, they dragged the heavy sack outside. Spangles snatched Vinegar's moped keys from the counter as they passed. A few seconds of swift grunting later, they were speeding along the promenade back towards Sausage's boat, which was still moored to the pier.

Spangles grinned the delighted grin of the soon-to-be-rich as he swerved the moped through the evening funfair funsters, while Sausage inhaled the air of victory and also the air of fish stink from his beard.

By the time they had climbed back down their ladder and carried the sack of coffee and fishy riches aboard Sausage's boat, the search party had all but given up on the café.

Mayor Jackson kicked the scattered coffee beans across the floor in frustration. Freddie refused to be beaten and continued pacing the small café. The spilled coffee beans crunched beneath his feet as he stepped over the two half-deflated sacks. 'Wait a minute, did you look in these sacks?' he asked everyone, 'Weren't they full when we came in? Like that one,' he added, pointing to the third, still full, sack. 'And weren't there four?'

Without waiting for an answer, Freddie thrust a hand into the full sack and found, to his surprise, a heavy wooden bucket and, shortly afterwards, a second identical bucket.

After checking the remaining sacks were hiding nothing but coffee beans, they carried the two sloshing buckets to the kitchen, popped the lids off and poured the stinky contents into a large sink.

The stink from the sink was unbelievable.

Guy Walker couldn't believe his nose or his eyes. Floating amongst the dead fishies was his bag of money.

The Bitter End

Spangles McNasty and Sausage-face Pete had been sailing away from Bitterly Bay for over an hour before they felt confident they weren't being followed. Spangles could barely believe his good luck. 'I feels a song comin' on, **me old Sausage**,' he said as he lowered the telescope again, satisfied no one was chasing them.

'What a time that was, eh? I got given a

TUNNEL OF DOOM, it turned out to be an awful non-spangler, we fixed it right up, stole that guy's **funny money**, nearly got ghostly, got sauced, got trapped by a **loopy** lady, got away and got rich!'

'When you puts it like that, it is **deffo worth a song**,' Sausage grinned from behind the steering wheel and beneath his fake whiskers. '**Spot of sushi** with the **singing**? We 'ave plenty right 'ere, **me old fish head**,' he said, kicking the coffee-bean sack with an excitable yellow welly.

'Ow!' the coffee-bean sack shouted at him.

'What's that, Sausage?' Spangles asked. 'Just slosh it out on deck there – we can eat it off the floor while we counts that **funny money**.'

'It spoke,' Sausage said, nervously.

'Oh. The funny money that talks. What did it say?' Spangles asked.

'It said, "Ow!"' Sausage looked more worried as the sack started to shake.

Spangles stared at the sack. The sack they had chosen because Sausage said it smelt of fish. The hoo-ba-ding-dongs suddenly froze his mind cogs. He leant closer to Sausage and smelt his stinky beard.

'You know when you sniffed this sack back in the café, Sausage, and declared it full of stinky sushi fish, you couldn't have perhaps just been smellin' your own filthy fishy whiskers there, could you? And maybe this 'ere is the sack with no fishies at all . . . the one with . . .'

Suddenly the sack erupted before their eyes as Vinegar Jones leapt up, clutching two fists full of Badass Bitter Roast and said, 'Coffee, anyone?'

Spangles McNasty screamed so loud Mayor Jackson heard him back on the pier in Bitterly Bay.

He had just finished helping the fire brigade fence off the disastrous end of the pier with yellow-and-black stripy tape that read:

ACTUAL FOR-REAL DANGER, NO FUN AT ALL. DO NOT ENTER.

This was not quite the ending the Mayor had hoped for, but at least Guy Walker got his money back and no one was hurt.

He gazed out to sea as the sun got its colouring pens out and scribbled bright orange all over the horizon of his favourite bay in all the world.

Mayor Jackson liked to think that if you made a wish watching the sun set over the sea it would come true. He wished that wherever Spangles McNasty and Sausage-face Pete had gone, they would like it so much they'd never come back.

Freddie, Tommy the Ghost and Wendy McKenzie heard the distant scream too. They were rocking gently in their seats at the top of the Biggish Wheel again, Freddie trying once more to overcome his FEAR of heights. It wasn't working and the faint scream didn't help, but at least it made him open his eyes. 'What was that?' he said, although he had a feeling it was the kind of scream a nutty nasty might do when he discovered he'd taken the wrong sack during his sail-away getaway.

'That, my friend, was the **ghost** of the funfair,' said Tommy, adding a quick **'WHOOOOOO'** to end the statement and pronounce it sound and true wisdom from beyond.

'Don't be daft, Tommy,' Wendy said. 'There's no such thing as ghosts.'

'What does that make me, then?' Tommy said stubbornly.

'Daft,' Wendy and Freddie said together, and laughed.

'So what's your uncle going to do with the **PILE OF DOOM**?' Freddie asked, looking at the remains of the roller coaster and hoping Spangles wouldn't attempt to rebuild it any time soon.

'He said the Council would have to sell the remains of the ride for scrap to pay for the repairs to the pier. Then he started rambling on about planning permission to build a hotel or something. Anyway, there's nothing left for Spangles McNasty if he ever comes back.'

Freddie thought this over and nodded his approval. He looked out over Bitterly Bay. It really was quite possibly the best-est, beautiful-est and oddest town on the planet of Earth.

It was a super-hot sunny evening in Bitterly Bay as the sun slipped behind the watery horizon for a well-earned rest. In fact the sun was in such a good mood after watching the day's shenanigans, it kept on shining all week.

A week in which Wendy McKenzie tried, failed and finally gave up trying to persuade TOMMY THE GHOST he was alive and well and not in the least bit ghostly.

Freddie tried, failed and gave up trying to overcome his **FEAR** of heights.

Fat Tony and Tony Two-scoops became so engrossed in their latest food fight on Bitterly Beach they didn't notice the tide coming in until their vans were almost completely underwater. They decided to give up fighting, be friends and open a new van together, called Hey Fatty Two-scoops.

Mayor Jackson became increasingly happy. He was very happy the **TUNNEL OF DOOM** was gone, making way eventually, he hoped, for his hotel. He was extremely happy Spangles McNasty had not returned, but most of all he was very extremely happy to finally take delivery of a particularly precious item he had wanted to exhibit in Bitterly Museum for a long time.

It was also a week in which Spangles McNasty disappeared.

Where did he go?

Nobody knew.

Where did he come from?

Bitterly Bay, but that's not particularly important right now.

What was his favourite pizza?

Calzone, but no one knew that either, except Franco from Bitterly Pizza Hot and he hadn't seen Spangles for ages.

In fact no one had seen Spangles McNasty or Sausage-face Pete or Vinegar Jones all week, not even the sun.

But the moon had.

If only the moon could somehow tell the sun, but they weren't really that close.

While all of Bitterly Bay slept soundly in their beds at night, the moon watched Spangles, Sausage and Vinegar slip quietly back into the harbour aboard Sausage's fishing boat, now disguised as a pirate ship. It watched as Spangles waved a fond farewell to the weirdest lady he'd ever met, hoping he'd see her again sometime. It watched as Spangles collected his camper van and hid that on the boat too.

The moon was still watching when Spangles strolled out on deck alone.

Spangles liked to count the stars when he couldn't sleep. Secretly, although even he realised it was impossible, he wanted to collect them all.

He'd just had a nightcap of Badass Bitter Roast with Sausage-face Pete, who had told him a real spangler of a tale. No wonder he couldn't sleep.

He said his auntie's dog's friend's owner's mum's sister's friend's cat's dad's owner's wife's brother-in-law's cousin was called Marjory and she worked for the Mayor.

And this Marjory had said the Mayor was about to take delivery of a very spangly thing indeed. A thing called the Diamond Skull.

Spangles did not know what a Diamond Skull

was but just the sound of it gave him the hoo-ba-doo-dars like never before and he decided at once he had to have it.

He took a deep breath of the cool sea air, looked up at the diamond-studded sky and winked at the moon.

'You know what I think, me old moon beam?' he asked the cheesy look-a-like. Spangles waited a polite second or two for the moon to reply but the moon wasn't listening, it was busy playing with the tide. 'Tomorrow's going to be a right super spangler of a day,' he grinned. 'I can just feel it.'

THE END

Steve Webb

Illustrated by Chris Mould

Spangles McNasty is convinced that he can get rich quick by stealing goldfish – after all, aren't they made of solid gold? Together with his friend Sausage-face Pete, he decides to find the great Fish of Gold. Only young Freddie Taylor can stop Spangles' dastardly plan, in a tale full of time-travelling jet skis, madcap chases and haunted custard.

'Unadulterated fun!'
Lovereading

'Ludicrous and funny'
BookTrust

9781783444007   £6.99

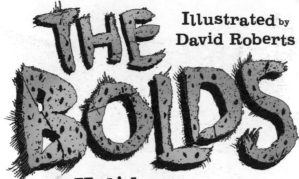

THE BOLDS

Illustrated by David Roberts

on Holiday

By Julian Clary

The Bolds may look ordinary, but they have a great big secret – they're hyenas!

It's the summer holidays, and the Bolds are going to camp by the sea. But it's not long before trouble sniffs them out, and one of them goes missing. Can the Bolds come to the rescue and carry on camping?

Praise for *The Bolds*

'Joyful'
Telegraph

'Glorious'
Daily Mail

'Heaps of fun'
Heat

9781783445066